# Oh no! Where is the sea?

Written by Rebecca Adlard

Illustrated by Nathalie Ortega

## Collins

# What is in this book?

Listen and say

beach

Download the audio at www.collins.co.uk/839678

sea

# The sea goes in ...

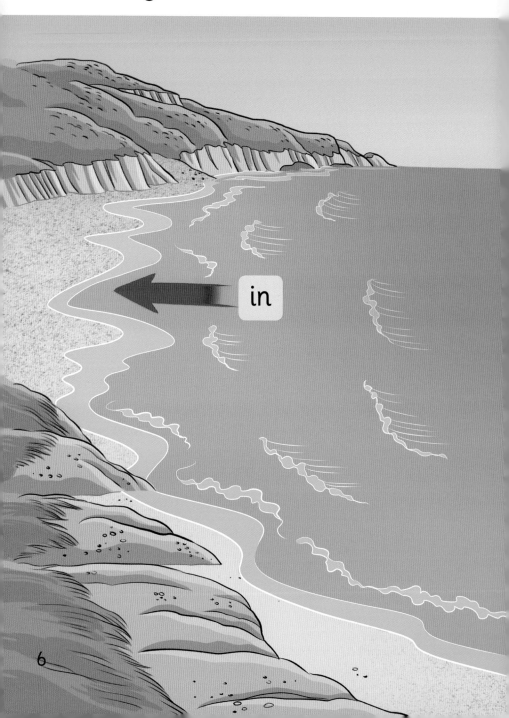

6

... and out.

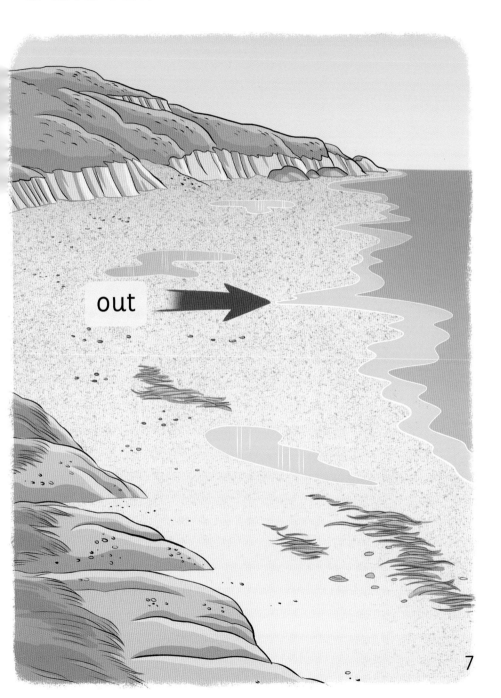

The sea is out. We see the sand.

We see the black rocks.

rocks

sand

Look! A rockpool. What is in the rockpool?

Lots of animals live in rockpools.

Look! An orange starfish.
It has got five arms.

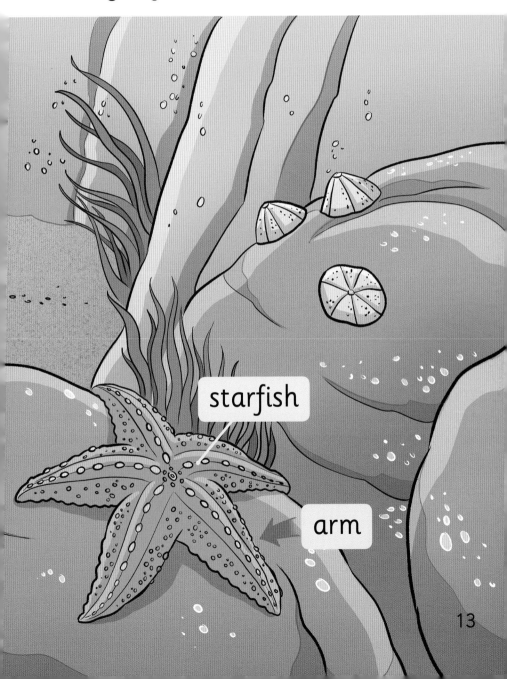

starfish

arm

# What is in the sand?

Look! A crab.

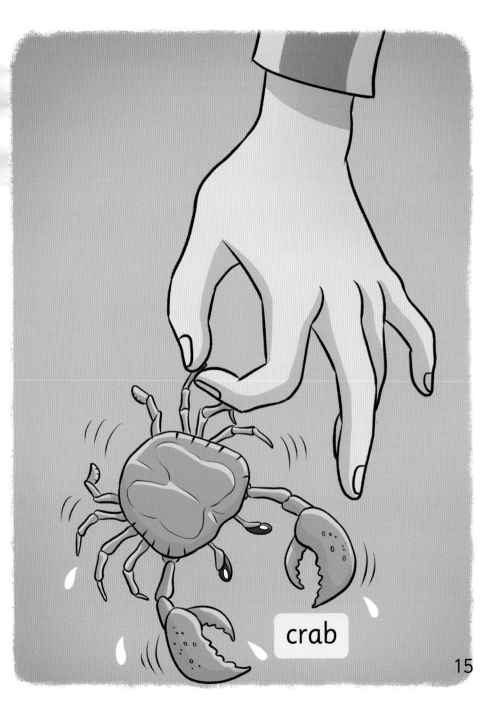

crab

15

We see seaweed and shells on
the beach.

seaweed

shell

Animals live in shells. Look!
Here is a crab in a shell.

The sea is out. We play on the sand.

The sea comes in.

# Picture dictionary

Listen and repeat

crab

fish

rockpool

sand

seaweed

shell

starfish

**1** Look and match

sea

beach

rockpool

**2** Listen and say

# Collins

Published by Collins
An imprint of HarperCollins*Publishers*
Westerhill Road
Bishopbriggs
Glasgow
G64 2QT

HarperCollins*Publishers*
1st Floor, Watermarque Building
Ringsend Road
Dublin 4
Ireland

William Collins' dream of knowledge for all began with the publication of his first book in 1819.

A self-educated mill worker, he not only enriched millions of lives, but also founded a flourishing publishing house. Today, staying true to this spirit, Collins books are packed with inspiration, innovation and practical expertise. They place you at the centre of a world of possibility and give you exactly what you need to explore it.

© HarperCollins*Publishers* Limited 2020

10 9 8 7 6 5 4 3 2

ISBN 978-0-00-839678-7

Collins® and COBUILD® are registered trademarks of HarperCollins*Publishers* Limited

www.collins.co.uk/elt

British Library Cataloguing in Publication Data

A catalogue record for this publication is available from the British Library.

Author: Rebecca Adlard
Illustrator: Nathalie Ortega (Beehive)
Series editor: Rebecca Adlard
Publishing manager: Lisa Todd
Product managers: Jennifer Hall and Caroline Green
In-house editor: Alma Puts Keren
Project manager: Emily Hooton
Editor: Rebecca Adlard
Proofreaders: Natalie Murray and Michael Lamb
Cover designer: Kevin Robbins
Typesetter: 2Hoots Publishing Services Ltd
Audio produced by id audio, London
Reading guide author: Emma Wilkinson
Production controller: Rachel Weaver
Printed and bound by: GPS Group, Slovenia

**MIX**
Paper from
responsible sources

FSC
www.fsc.org

**FSC™ C007454**

Download the audio for this book and a reading guide for parents and teachers at www.collins.co.uk/839678